APPLE  CIDER PUP

ISBN 978-0-692-50018-7

Printed in the United States of America
Printed on the Espresso Book Machine at Michigan State University

First Printing, 2015

APPLE CIDER PUP

WRITTEN BY
DONNA RUBIN

ILLUSTRATED BY
MARANDA ZIMMERMAN

East Lansing, Michigan
2015

Dedicated to all the apples of my eye from Texas to Michigan. Their fruitful support and encouragement has made this pie in the sky project a delicious dream come true.

-DONNA

Dedicated to my daughter Marceline Ann who sat, slept and wiggled on my lap during this whole puppy project.

-MARANDA

I'm the Apple Cider Pup.

Come join me for a cup,

As we visit cider mills

From long, long ago.

Woof, woof! My name is Puppy Appleseed and I want to take you to some of the apple cider mills* and orchards* of Michigan. With more than 100 cider mills and over 1000 apple orchards, we can only "pawse" to visit a few of them today. As we meander* along you will learn lots of apple terms, facts and a few recipes.

*Look in the glossary at the back of this book for "applelicious" terms. I hope you have a doggone good time on our trip.

Puppy Appleseed Fact:

Apples were first grown from seeds by the Greeks and Romans. Later, Europeans grafted* apples and brought seedlings* to America, since only small, sour, wild crab apples were native crops. The first American apple orchard was planted in Massachusetts in 1630.

I'm the Apple Cider Pup.

Come join me for a cup,

As we visit cider mills

From long, long ago.

Bark, bark, woof! Our first stop, the historic Franklin Cider Mill, was built in 1837, the same year Michigan became a state. It's fun to watch water from the Rouge River splash over the giant candy-apple-red metal wheel that turns the press to squeeze apples into sweet cider. Every Labor Day the mill opens for 100 days to enjoy brown paper bags full of hot, delicious doughnuts and jugs of crisp, cold cider while sitting along the river's edge. I like to dip my doughnut into the cider, but then my paws get sticky, so I just have to keep on licking.

Lick, lick, mmmm.

Puppy Appleseed Fact:

From 1795 to 1845 John Chapman, fondly known as Johnny Appleseed, planted apple seeds he gathered from cider presses* in Ohio, Indiana, Illinois and Pennsylvania. Who knows, he could have even visited the Franklin Cider Mill to get some of his seeds. Johnny Appleseed was a gentle person, loved by animals and frontier* folks because he provided food through the harsh winters. I like to imagine myself as a distant relative to Johnny.

I'm the Apple Cider Pup.

Come join me for a cup,

As we visit Yates Cider Mill

From long, long ago.

In Rochester, Michigan, we spot the 1863 Yates Mill from far away with its large red barn and working water wheel. The Clinton River spins their 100 year old water turbine* to press apples. The folks at Yates are so dog gone friendly they allow dogs to take their masters on walks along their Clinton river trail. Be sure to try one of my favorite treats, a Yates cider donut ice cream sundae with caramel sauce. It's easy for me to lick it right out of the bowl, but you humans can use a spoon if you must.
Yip, yip hooray!

Puppy Appleseed Fact: <u>How a Cider Press Works</u>

1. Select a variety of sweet and tart apples.

2. Clean and wash apples.

3. Grind apples into bits.

4. Layer 1000 chopped apples on nylon blankets.

5. Squeeze juice with 50 tons of pressure* from cider press.

6. Pour cider into a tank to cool.

7. Pump into jugs, ready to sell.

I'm the Apple Cider Pup.

Come join me for a cup,

As we visit apple orchards

From long, long ago.

Sniff, sniff. Following my nose we find Miller's Big Red Apple Orchard, the oldest apple orchard in Washington Township. Let's take a hayride and pick our own apples right off the trees. My paws are too short to reach, but you would do a fine job picking bushels* of fresh apples, peaches, berries and cherries. Hop aboard for a waggin' good time.

Just a shake of a hound's tail away in Romeo, Michigan, is Blake's Orchard and Cider Mill. On Blake's 500 acres of farmland, we fetch apples, pumpkins, pears or even Christmas trees. It's fun to pretend I'm a hound dog from long ago as we rumble into their orchard on a tractor. Those farms dogs sure had the life...a dog's life, that is.

Puppy Appleseed Fact:

Each season has a purpose for growing apples. In winter the trees become dormant* and rest. When spring warms the ground, pink and white buds burst open on the branches and fill the air with a sweet fragrance. These blossoms turn into young, green apples that grow all summer long. Fall is harvest time when ripe, juicy apples are handpicked, cleaned and sorted. Finally, they are shipped to factories, stores or cider mills for us to enjoy.

One of my favorite things to cook after picking apples is yummy, warm applesauce. It tastes much fresher than the store-bought kind. You can use any variety of apples, tart or sweet, just be sure they are from Michigan, as well as the cider and maple syrup. We sure are lucky pups to live in a land that is chock full of crops and other gifts from Mother Nature. Let's get cooking!

Michigan Maple Applelicious Applesauce
Always have adult help when cooking.

12 Michigan apples, any variety
1 cup Michigan apple cider
½ cup Michigan maple syrup
¼ cup lemon juice
1 tablespoon ground cinnamon

Wash, peel, and core apples and slice into 2-inch chunks. Place into a deep cooking pot. Toss apples with lemon juice to prevent browning. Pour in apple cider and maple syrup and sprinkle cinnamon over the top. Bring everything to a simmer then cover and cook over low heat for 30 minutes. Crush mixture with a potato masher and cook on low uncovered for 20 more minutes or until soft. Stir gently to prevent the applesauce from sticking to the pot. Let cool before eating, but Puppy Appleseed likes to lap this up while it is still warm. Yummy!

I'm the Apple Cider Pup.

Come join me for a cup,

As we visit Spicer Orchards

From long, long ago.

Visiting Spicer Orchards feels like a fall festival where you can weigh your own pumpkins, buy fresh popped kettle corn and local honey made by the apple tree bees. I like to snuggle up beside the blacksmith's* fire and watch him forge* metal tools on a cold, crisp day. It's lots of fun for kiddos to have their faces painted or eat a caramel apple on a stick...just like they might find at any local fair. There's a full day of dog gone good fun at our cider mills in Michigan. Oh, don't forget to come hungry; hot dogs are my favorite. They're grrrrreat!

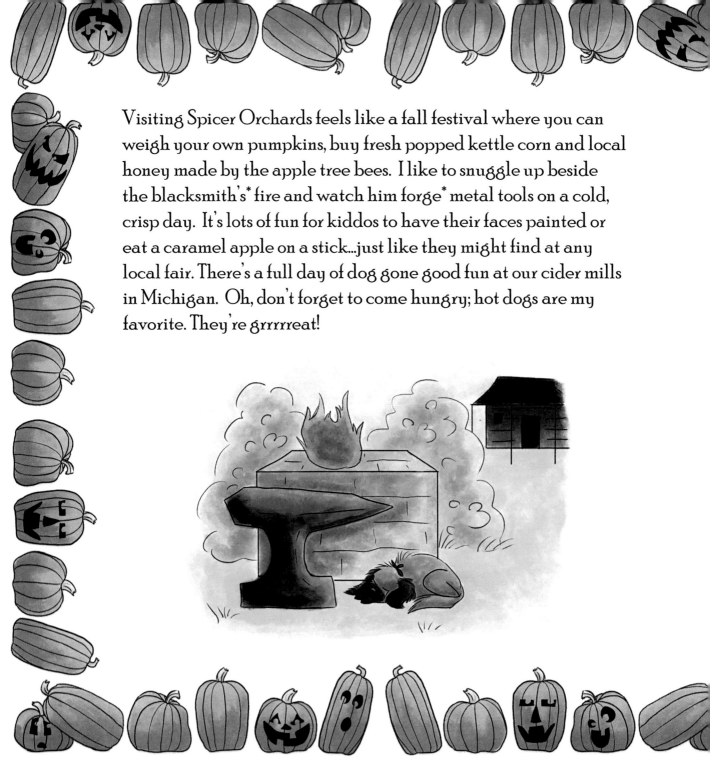

Puppy Appleseed Fact:

If it weren't for honeybees we would not have yummy honey or apples. Beekeepers*
visit orchards every spring when pink apple blossoms are fully opened. As honey
bees drink nectar* they move from flower to flower. Yellow pollen clinging onto
their legs is carried from one blossom to another which pollinates* every apple tree
in the orchard.

I'm the Apple Cider Pup.

Come join me for a cup,

As we visit Uncle John's

From long, long ago.

Uncle John's Cider Mill in St. John's, Michigan, has been owned by the Beck family for five generations*. Uncle John and Aunt Carolyn converted their old cattle barn into a two-story cider mill where they make award winning apple cider and lots of home baked goodies. With antique* car shows and craft festivals there is always fun for every age at Uncle John's. My ears always perk up to the live music played on the weekends. When they start to sing, "How Much is That Doggy in the Window?" I can't help but wag my tail and howl along. Ow ooh!

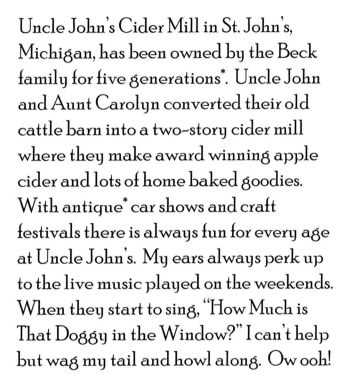

Puppy Appleseed Fact:

Everyone on the apple farm has to pitch in at harvest time. Apples are hand picked from trees so they do not bruise. Thick cloth bags worn around the pickers' shoulders have a special bottom flap that unsnaps to empty apples into bins when full. Many wooden bins are stored in big cooling houses until ready to eat, sell or squeeze into cider.

I'm the Apple Cider Pup.

Come join me for a cup,

As we tour Robinette's Apple Haus

From long, long ago.

Close to Grand Rapids, Michigan, we find another cider mill that has been family owned for generations. Since 1911, the Robinette family has operated an apple orchard with a bakery, gift shop and winery in their old wooden barns. One of my favorite pastimes at cider mills is exploring corn mazes*; giant puzzles that are planted and cut in a cornfield by a tractor. Since the corn is too tall to see over, it is easy to get lost in loops and dead ends in the maze. Lucky for my master and me, there's a map to help us navigate* our way to the finish line. At Robinette's maze, we answer corn trivia* questions to guide us down the right paths. Personally, I just give an extra loud bark to get all the help I need to find my way safely to the end of the maze. Woof! Woof!

Puppy Appleseed Fact:

The three top apple-growing states in the U.S. are Washington, New York and Michigan. The United States is the second largest apple-producing nation, just behind China, producing over 200 million bushels of apples yearly. The average person in the United States eats over 42 pounds of apples and apple products every year. Perhaps Michiganders eat even more than the average apple amount.

I'm the Apple Cider Pup.

Come join me for a cup,

As we visit Dexter Cider Mill

From long, long ago.

Along the winding Huron River, we come across the oldest cider mill in Michigan. The folks at the Dexter Cider Mill still squeeze their apples with a one hundred year old oak cider press and display a hand-operated one similar to the kind colonists* used during Johnny Appleseed's days. The Dexter Mill is a fall favorite for river canoeists who stop off for a cup of cider, hand rolled gingersnaps, frozen cider slushes or apple strudel. Their award winning apple cookbook is always for sale at the mill, but I have included my own secret recipe for apple pie. Mmm, mmm, good.

Puppy Appleseed Fact:

Apples are nutritious*, full of fiber and vitamins. Eating an apple, often called nature's toothbrush, can help clean your teeth and gums. Yummy apple products include: apple cider, apple juice, apple pie, apple bread, applesauce, apple butter, apple cider vinegar, caramel and candied apples, apple strudel and dried apples. Some folks call it nature's perfect fruit and I agree. What do you think?

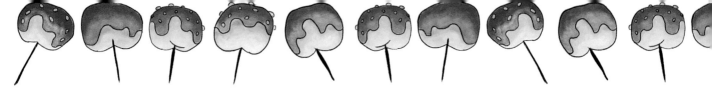

Puppy Appleseed's Apple Pie

Remember to always have adult supervision when cooking.

Ingredients:
1 package refrigerated ready-made piecrusts
6-8 cooking apples such as Granny Smith or Honey crisp
1 tablespoon lemon juice
½ cup sugar
2 tablespoons flour
1 teaspoon cinnamon
2 tablespoons cold butter cut into cubes
1 egg
2 pinches cinnamon and 1 tablespoon sugar mixed together

Procedure:
Preheat oven to 400 degrees. Line a 9 inch pie plate with one ready-made piecrust. Peel, core and slice the apples into large chunks. Place the apples in a bowl and toss with lemon juice. Combine sugar, flour, and cinnamon and add to the apples. Mix well to coat apples. Pour into crust lined pie plate, piling apples high in the center. Dot the apples with cubed butter. Top with the second crust and pinch the crust edges to seal. Cut slits in the top piecrust to release steam. Beat the egg and brush it over the top crust. Sprinkle the top with cinnamon and sugar mixture. Bake for 50 minutes until apples are tender and crust is evenly browned. Serve warm with ice cream or a thin slice of cheddar cheese on top.

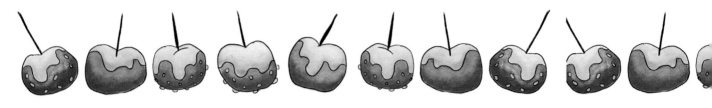

It has been such fun traveling across Michigan with you and stopping at several of our local cider mills. I hope you have learned some interesting facts about apples and how they are grown and harvested*. There are many more cider mills to explore in our apple adventure land of Michigan, so get a move on, you'll have a howling good time...
I doggone guarantee it.

GLOSSARY

Antique: of or belonging to the past

Beekeeper: a person who raises honeybees

Blacksmith: a person who makes objects from iron

Bushel: a unit of dry measure equal to 4 pecks

Cider Mill: a place that extracts juice from apples to make cider

Cider Press: a flat press for crushing chopped apples into cider

Colonists: an inhabitant of the 13 British colonies that became the U.S.A.

Dormant: in a state of rest or inactivity

Forge: to form iron by heating and hammering

Frontier: the 19th century period of the western settlement of the U.S.A.

Gallon: a unit of liquid measure equal to 4 quarts

Generation: the offspring of a parent or couple

Graft: to insert a shoot of one plant into the stem of another plant

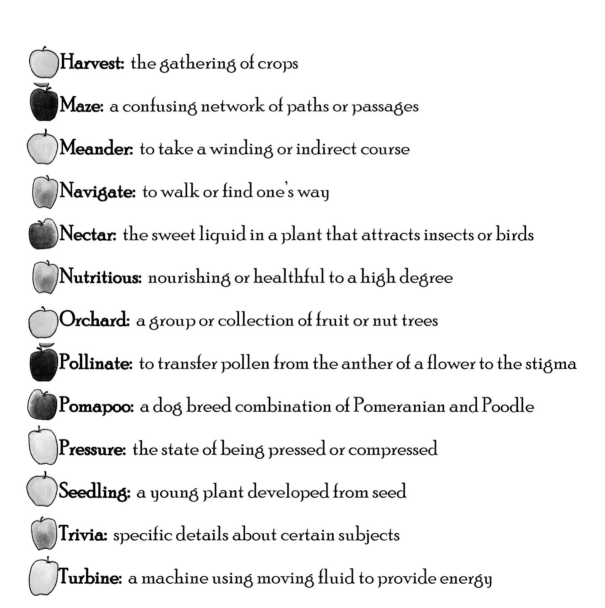

Harvest: the gathering of crops

Maze: a confusing network of paths or passages

Meander: to take a winding or indirect course

Navigate: to walk or find one's way

Nectar: the sweet liquid in a plant that attracts insects or birds

Nutritious: nourishing or healthful to a high degree

Orchard: a group or collection of fruit or nut trees

Pollinate: to transfer pollen from the anther of a flower to the stigma

Pomapoo: a dog breed combination of Pomeranian and Poodle

Pressure: the state of being pressed or compressed

Seedling: a young plant developed from seed

Trivia: specific details about certain subjects

Turbine: a machine using moving fluid to provide energy

www.blakefarms.com

www.robinettes.com

www.dextercidermill.com

www.spicerorchards.com

www.franklincidermill.com

www.ujcidermill.com

www.millersbigred.com

www.yatescidermill.com

About the Author

Donna Rubin enjoys visiting the cider mills of Michigan with her trained therapy dog, Pax, a rescued Pomapoo*. As an educator, Donna is a lifelong learner of local history and food who shares her love for the "mitten" with students of all ages with her puppet, Puppy Appleseed. Contact them for author visits and more delicious apple cider news at:

www.appleciderpup.com

About the Illustrator

Maranda Zimmerman is an art student studying Computer Graphics Animation. She enjoys creating stories and various animal characters, but especially dogs. When not imagining, she likes to spend time with her family and her pit bull Cletus.

www.facebook.com/artbymaranda